PRAIRIE DOG TOWN

SMITHSONIAN
WILD HERITAGE COLLECTION

For Marvin
    — B.R.

To my father, Everett,
for his example of intelligence,
ability and social consciousness
    — D.H.

Copyright © 1993 by Trudy Management Corporation,
165 Water Street, Norwalk, CT 06856, and the Smithsonian Institution,
Washington, DC 20560.

Book Design: Johanna P. Shields

First Edition
10 9 8 7 6 5 4 3 2 1
Printed in Singapore

Library of Congress Cataloging-in-Publication Data

Rogers, Bettye. 1934-

Prairie dog town / by Bettye Rogers :
illustrated by Deborah Howland.
            p.   cm.
Summary: Unable to find enough food in the community where he has grown
up, Prairie Dog crosses the prairie to an area with more vegetation and digs a
burrow of his own.
        ISBN 1-56899-005-7
1. Prairie dogs — Juvenile fiction. [1. Prairie dogs — Fiction.]
I. Howland, Deborah, ill. II. Title.
        PZ10.3.R626Pr   1993   93-13357
        (E) — dc20   CIP
                                                                     AC

02

1993

BRITISH BOOK DONATION TO FLOOD TOWNS

**British Government helps flooded towns
in midwest replace school library books**

PRAIRIE DOG TOWN

by Bettye Rogers
Illustrated by Deborah Howland

Soundprints

A Division of Trudy Management Corporation
Norwalk, Connecticut

Spring's gentle rain falls, turning the prairie lush and green. The yearling Prairie Dog and his large family grow plump and sleek from the choice young grasses and other plants thriving in their territory.

But all too soon these spring days pass, and summer comes. For weeks there is no rain. The sun shines hot each day and bakes the prairie dry. Grasses and flowers shrivel and turn brown.

At dawn, in a sleeping room deep underground, Prairie Dog wakes up. Stretching, he shakes pieces of dry grass from his fur and listens. His brothers and sisters, still sleeping, breathe softly. His mother murmurs as she begins to wake up. Wide awake, his father scrambles up the tunnel to the sentry post.

Prairie Dog is hungry. And
so he scurries up the steep tunnel
after his father. He stops before the
entrance to listen and sniff. It seems
safe so he peeks out. He sees his
father, sitting on his haunches on
the mound above. "Yek-yek-yek," his
father barks the "all clear" signal.
It is safe to go outside.

Prairie Dog blinks in the bright, orange sunlight. He sees many reddish-brown heads with bright eyes and small ears pop out of tunnels. As day begins, Prairie Dog hears the noisy chatter of his busy town.

He greets his father, an aunt and two cousins. They greet each other and "kiss" by rubbing their noses and teeth together. They groom one another, using their front paws to scratch through each other's fur.

Then Prairie Dog scampers down from the mound to search his family's territory for food. The grass stems he clips are dry. He digs for roots and munches on prickly pear cactus. He finds some insects to eat, but it is not enough. He is still hungry.

Prairie Dog is not the only one who is hungry. While he is nibbling on a dry leaf, a dark shadow suddenly passes overhead. He chirps wildly to warn others about the dangerous hunting hawk, and then tumbles over backward in his own rush to the safety of his den.

His warning call is repeated all over town, "churk-churk-churk." Furry bodies dive into safe burrows and wait for the "all clear."

Prairie Dog's father waits in the "listening room" of the family's burrow. When he peeks out, the hawk has gone. He climbs onto the mound and gives the all-clear signal. It is repeated around the town.

Soon Prairie Dog, his family and neighbors come back above ground, and there is nosing and kissing, rolling and tussling, grooming and scampering all around the town.

Prairie Dog and a sister both grab for the same grass stem. They tug, and it falls apart. They wrestle and roll into one of the many holes dug in the family's territory to find roots.

Each day food is harder to find. But Prairie Dog is old enough to move beyond the crowded town to a place where there is more food.

There are no streets in this town. To find open prairie, he must cross many territories belonging to other families. He creeps carefully among the mounds, stopping often to check for danger. Sometimes, a warning "churr" sends him scurrying out of one family's territory into another's. On his journey he is an intruder everywhere.

At the end of the day, Prairie Dog shivers in the quickly cooling air. Tonight for the first time, he will not be in his safe home. With his sharp claws Prairie Dog quickly digs a shallow nest for shelter.

There are new dangers at dusk as night hunters begin searching for their supper. A coyote howls. Frantic alarms are barked when a rare black-footed ferret is spotted among the mounds.

In the pink dawn he wakes up and listens. A burrowing owl's wings whoosh softly as it settles on its mound. A rattlesnake rustles the grass as it slithers past. Prairie Dog does not move on until all is quiet.

At last he comes to an open, grassy stretch of prairie. Other yearling males have safely come this far, too. They feast on blue gramma and buffalo grasses. Then they begin to dig new burrows.

Prairie Dog digs a tunnel
with his strong forefeet, kicking dirt
out with his hind feet. As he gets
deeper, he turns and pushes dirt out
with his forearms. Branching off the
tunnel, he digs a listening room, a
bedroom, a toilet and an emergency
exit that is also an air vent. He
hollows out a special room where
he will be safe from floods.

He uses his nose to press the dirt from his tunnel into a firm mound around the entrance. It will protect his burrow against flash floods. Then he cuts the grasses and plants around the mound, so he can see his enemies clearly.

He carpets his bedroom with soft grasses. When winter comes, he will be snug and safe in his new home below the prairie.

About the Black-tailed Prairie Dog

When early European explorers encountered prairie dogs on the American continent they gave them the name petit chien, *meaning little dog. At that time, there were billions of prairie dogs living on the great plains of the western United States. These social little rodents lived in huge "towns" that extended for many miles in all directions. Today the prairie dogs still live in towns, but their numbers and territories have dwindled due to disease and the destruction of their natural habitat.*

Glossary

burrow: a hole in the ground dug by an animal for shelter or to live in. Prairie dogs are known to be among the best burrowing and engineering animals.

kiss: referring to the way prairie dogs greet and identify each other. When familiar prairie dogs meet, they open their mouths and touch teeth together.

sentry post: a place on the mound surrounding the prairie dog burrow from which the prairie dog watches for danger.

territory: area within the town where a prairie dog family lives. Each family group protects its territory by keeping non-family members out.

yearling: a prairie dog that is more than one year old and less than two years old.

Points of Interest in this Book

p. 9 oil beetle; yellow bumble bee.

pp. 12-13 a prairie dog's primary diet is vegetation — grasses and broad-leaved weeds. The prairie dog will also eat insects such as grasshoppers and cutworms to provide protein.

p. 13 grasshopper.

pp. 14-15 hawks are only one of the prairie dog's predators. Others include eagles, coyote, bobcats, foxes, badgers and the black-footed ferret.

pp. 18-19 the boundaries of a prairie dog town change from time to time in response to disease, the abundance of food and changes in weather.

pp. 24-25 prairie dogs and burrowing owls commonly live side by side. The owls make their homes in burrows abandoned by prairie dogs.

p. 25 Western diamondback rattlesnake.

p. 27 thistle; purple coneflower; American painted ladies.

pp. 28-29 a typical burrow has several rooms branching off from the main tunnel. These rooms include a sleeping room, a nursery, a toilet, a listening room, and an air chamber to be used in case of flooding. Each burrow also has at least one secondary exit to allow for fresh air. This exit can also be used in case of an emergency.